STAR WARS
RETURN OF THE JEDI ™

The Adventures of Teebo

A TALE of MAGIC and SUSPENSE

Written and Illustrated by
Joe Johnston

Random House 🏠 New York

Cover art by Jan Brett

TM and © 1984 Lucasfilm Ltd. (LFL). All rights reserved under International and Pan-American Copyright Conventions. Published in the United States by Random House, Inc., New York, and simultaneously in Canada by Random House of Canada Limited, Toronto.

Library of Congress Cataloging in Publication Data:
Johnston, Joe. The adventures of Teebo. SUMMARY: Teebo the daydreaming Ewok finds the peace of his village destroyed when Vulgarr the Dulok reports that Teebo's sister, Malani, has been stolen by the giant Grudakk. [1. Fantasy] I. Title PZ7.J6442Ad 1984 [Fic] 83-24686 ISBN: 0-394-86568-5 (trade); 0-394-96568-X (lib. bdg.)
Manufactured in the United States of America   1 2 3 4 5 6 7 8 9 0

In a far corner of the universe, on one of the forest moons of the planet Endor, there lived a tribe of small furry folk called Ewoks. In a village perched high in the branches of the ancient trees they lived happy lives, with love and goodwill for their fellow Ewoks and deep respect for the Great Spirit of the forest.

As soon as an Ewok baby could walk, he began to learn about the forest world around him, about the family of trees and sky and soil and Ewoks, and about the Forest Father who watched over all. In long processions the children of the village marched the forest floor and high walkways, guided and tutored by the Ewok elders.

One of these young Ewoks was named Teebo. Teebo lived with his parents and his little sister, Malani, in a cozy hut of three chambers just off the village square. As normal Ewok children go, Teebo wasn't. Of course, he looked normal, with his brindle-brown fur and sparkling green eyes. He did normal chores, like caring for the tree that was planted on the day of his birth and thatching the walls of the family hut. Like all young Ewoks, Teebo knew the strange, unspoken language of the trees, and he especially loved to listen to all the Ewok legends that he would someday pass on to his own children.

But Teebo was different. He would spend hours sitting on his secret high branch in one of the oldest trees in the grove. In his perch he could daydream and watch the rivers of color that flowed across the sky. The sky colors seemed to sing a bright song to the forest below, but sometimes Teebo wasn't sure if he heard the songs or just felt them move past him like a stream flowing over smooth rocks. In these songs Teebo could hear different voices. He could sense the happiness when the voices rejoiced at the planting of a new birth-tree, and the sorrow when the voices mourned the end of a tree's lifetime.

When Teebo told his friends about the rivers of color, they laughed and made up funny rhymes about him and seldom invited him to join in their adventures. They said he must have fallen out of his tree house and landed on his head. Teebo never told them about the sky songs or reading the animals' minds or seeing the tree ghost. He didn't mind the laughter; he just wished someone could share his secret world. Teebo's parents decided he simply had a spirited imagination.

This, at least, was true. Teebo loved to daydream—perhaps a little more than was good for him. When the other Ewok children were learning how to make weapons to defend Happy Grove or which vines were safe to swing on or how the wings of their gliders worked, Teebo would sit in a daze, imagining himself doing battle with monsters or rescuing baby Ewoks from danger or flying high into the night sky to collect basketfuls of stars. "Teebo the Great!" the Ewoks would cheer as he sprinkled stars throughout the grove to light the village by night. "Hooray for Teebo!"

One brisk afternoon in the time of year we would call

spring, the Ewok children were gathering for another excursion into the forest. Suddenly three Duloks came stomping into the village square, making such a racket that even Teebo was roused from his afternoon daydreaming.

Now first a word about Duloks. Although Duloks were distant relatives of the Ewoks, the two tribes had little in common. Whereas Ewoks were kind, sensitive, brave, and industrious, Duloks seemed to pride themselves on their rudeness and dishonesty. Most Duloks were lanky and ill-proportioned, with wide jowls and beady eyes. Verminous, patchy gray fur concealed their mottled pink underhides. Although the Ewoks tolerated the Duloks out of respect for the forest and all its inhabitants, there were many Ewok superstitions concerning Duloks. All in all, Ewoks avoided them whenever possible.

"Ewoks, Ewoks, to arms, to arms!" shouted the Dulok leader, whose name was Vulgarr. "A creature of dread has stolen one of your children. Look!" Vulgarr went to the rail and pointed down to the bank of the stream that wound through the Ewoks' grove. There in the mud, the prints of giant feet led off into the forest.

All the Ewoks in the village pushed fearfully to the railing and gasped. None among them had ever seen footprints so large before.

"I saw it all," said Vulgarr, raising his voice for attention. "The little one wore a red feather in her hood and carried this." Vulgarr held up a ragged Ewok doll made of straw. "The poor child dropped it when the wicked beast grabbed her."

Teebo's mother, whose name was Batcheela, fought

back tears; she knew the doll belonged to her daughter, Malani. Teebo's father, whose name was Warok, stepped forward.

"And why did you not raise an outcry, Vulgarr," he asked, "so that we might have attacked the creature?"

"I thought only of the child, of course," said the pompous Dulok. "She might have been injured had I interfered."

Chirpa, the chief of the village, turned to the Ewoks whose duty was defense of the grove. "I will take ten of the best archers. We will track down the beast and rescue the child."

At this, Vulgarr roared with laughter. "Ten Ewoks to slay such a giant? This long-haired monster is as big as a hut, with great fiery eyes and teeth as big as your hand and the strength of fifty Ewoks . . . at least! Many times I have seen this creature stalking the woodland in the dead of night. He makes his own trails, and his wrath is as awesome as his appetite. Trust me. It will take all of your warriors to subdue him. But do make haste. Like many creatures of the deep and dark, this monster may dine at dusk."

"Logray must guide us in matters such as this," said Arbo, the legend keeper. "He is oldest and wisest and is close to the ways of the Spirit. We will send for Logray!"

"By all means!" scoffed Vulgarr. "While the kidnapper travels league after league into the depths of the distant forest! Farewell, Ewoks. You have been forewarned."

"Wait, Vulgarr," called Chief Chirpa as he looked around the circle of nervous Ewok faces. "Elders, take all the children to the stronghouse and guard them well. Any and all warriors who would help slay the creature, make ready your wings. We must search while shadows are short."

"Ah, spoken like a wise warrior," said Vulgarr. "But why hunt in vain? As king of all Duloks, I range my forests far and broad. I know where this creature makes his lair."

"In truth, Ewoks seldom venture an arrow's flight from home and kin," said Chirpa. "Guide us then, Vulgarr, and name your reward."

Vulgarr recoiled in mock horror. "What!? The king of the Duloks sailing the treetops on wings of sticks and strings? Not likely. Follow the Whispering River to the Canyons of Mist. At the third bend, look high on the canyon wall. There in a cave dwells the beast. Fair winds to all." The three Duloks quickly took their leave.

Warok watched the trio depart. "Always and always the Duloks smirch our trails, play us their tricks, steal of our harvest. I have no trust for them."

"True to form, the Duloks gain from our labors," said Pondo, a younger warrior, "for the woods will be safer for Duloks as well after this creature is slain."

"Warriors, to your wings!" shouted Chief Chirpa. "Warok will lead us. Mates and elders, watch over the children. We fly!"

The warriors shuffled quickly down the launchway as mothers darted around scooping up their children. One by one, the winged warriors leaped into the air. Banking and swooping and pushing their flutter ropes, they rode the great currents of warm forest air up into the sunlight.

Logray, the Ewok medicine man, hobbled slowly along a walkway high in the treetops. Old beyond memory, he knew that he would soon join the Spirit and a younger

Ewok would take his place. Logray stopped to rest and watch the beckoning sky. Suddenly a line of flying Ewok warriors in full battle dress soared overhead, their legs pumping the kick ropes, their axes and clubs dangling. Summoning his strength, Logray hurried toward the village.

Meanwhile, the children were all being gathered into the central shelter. That is, all the children but one. Slipping free of the chattering crowd, Teebo hid in an overturned basket. From inside it he could see the last of the warriors leaping into the air. When the square was finally clear, Teebo crept across the village. His heart ached with dread at the thought of his captive sister, yet he trembled with excitement for the adventure to come.

Teebo raced to the racks of extra wings, picked a big, sturdy-looking pair, and strapped himself in. He had never actually flown before, but he had often watched the warriors practicing their landings and takeoffs. Slipping his feet into the kick loops, he flapped a couple of times. It wasn't easy to remember what the elders had said about banking and turning. It wasn't easy . . . Teebo had been watching the skyrivers of color that day.

With a last look around, Teebo ran a few hopping steps down the launchway and jumped. Out over the green cavern of forest he flew. A rising surge of air caught Teebo's quivering wings and lofted him up, up into the sunshine, up past the tops of trees. Teebo tugged and kicked and shifted his weight to no avail; he was too small and light to have much effect on the widespread wings. At the mercy of the wind, he watched in dismay as the

formation of flying warriors disappeared from view. Up he floated in his sunny blue world until he could see the whole forest spread out beneath him. At the curving horizon, land and sky merged softly in a blue-green haze. Higher still he drifted, up, up, up . . .

   When Logray entered the village square, Arbo rushed to tell him the story. The old medicine man stood silently looking at the sky with narrowed eyes, as if distant voices called to him. Finally he spoke: "You describe a creature very much like the Grudakk. Among living Ewoks, I alone have seen the Grudakk, and alone I must go to—"
   "Listen!" Batcheela interrupted. "The forest is as still as death, and in the air . . ."
   All the villagers sniffed and listened, but there was nothing to hear.
   "The Great Spirit has silenced his domain," said Logray. "Take warning. Danger approaches."
   Silence. Not even a leaf stirring in the breeze. Then . . . a cracking twig, a thud, a gruff curse, the crash of branches, and a scream. Vulgarr and thirty red-eyed Duloks swooped down from above on swinging vines. Whooping and hollering, they crashed into the midst of the startled villagers.
   Vulgarr shouted commands and swung a gnarled club of rootwood. Any Ewok, male or female, young or old, who passed within range was dealt a reeling blow.
   Batcheela grabbed a clay pot and crashed it down on the head of a scrawny gray Dulok, then seized him by the ankles and began to whirl. Two attackers caught unawares were sent tumbling over the railing to fall

yowling to the forest floor.

Just as Logray began to cast a spell on the marauders, Vulgarr sent his club skittering across the village square to knock the old Ewok onto his back. Then the Dulok sprang quickly and secured a bag of blue toadskin over Logray's head. Further spells were rendered harmless.

The villagers fought fiercely, but without their warriors they were no match for the long-armed Duloks. The battle was soon at an end. Dazed and bruised, the Ewoks were huddled together.

"Bind them well!" shouted a panting Vulgarr as he wiped the drool from his chin. "And now for our hard-won prize."

Vulgarr crashed into the stronghouse and, amid screams of terror, emerged with a baby Ewok. He lifted the wide-eyed wokling by the scruff of the neck for inspection.

"Not enough fur here to yield a berry pouch," said the leering Vulgarr, "but here's a meal fit for even me, the king of the Duloks." With screams of wicked glee the raiders pranced and capered, tossing the hapless infant to and fro. The villagers sat shaking with fear for the lives of their children.

"Oh, do not grieve, fine mothers," Vulgarr said with a laugh. "At least your warriors will return, unless the monster's ghost should get them!" Amid gales of Dulok laughter, two of Vulgarr's henchmen entered the square carrying a great slab of wood, hewn in the shape of a huge foot and covered with mud. "Here is your fearsome monster," cackled Vulgarr. The Duloks drove the children out into the square and corralled them together.

"Take them to the wagon!" shouted Vulgarr as the wind rose and the sky darkened. "And with haste . . . a storm is nigh!"

From under the hood of toadskin came the ominous voice of Logray. "It is no storm you fear. You have done the Spirit a terrible wrong. Return our young. Go your way or even the spell of the seven oaths will not shield you from the Great Spirit's wrath."

Vulgarr threw back his head and laughed an ugly, howling laugh as the wind lashed at the village and the sky churned. "I'll show you spells, wise man!" screamed Vulgarr, his eyes wild and staring. He raised his lumpy club and advanced on the bound and hooded Logray. The villagers gasped.

Suddenly a blue bolt of lightning leaped out of a cloud and severed a heavy branch high overhead. Vulgarr scrambled aside as the branch crashed through to the floor of the village on the very spot where he had been standing. It plummeted to the ground far below.

The Duloks ceased their laughter. Vulgarr shot a long, hateful look at the churning sky. Then he spun around and departed, followed by his nervous henchmen pushing the Ewok children before them.

With a last spiraling gust, the wind calmed and the sky cleared. The only sounds to be heard were the small sobs of the Ewok mothers.

Teebo drifted high above the ancient forest. Purple shadows of late afternoon began to crawl across the darkening land below. The sistermoon climbed the horizon and the first stars twinkled above, but to Teebo's dismay they appeared no closer than they did from his village. At the thought of the village Teebo searched the landscape for a river or a hill or something he might know, but nothing looked like home. To the west, Teebo saw a tree unlike any he had seen before. Its trunk spiraled up to scrape the passing clouds and beyond. Around its base, normal trees seemed to press close. He glided high above the tumbled ruins of what must have been a once mighty fortress. From fallen ramparts and dank portals, flitting gauzelike figures watched him pass.

The cooling air was slowly lowering Teebo into a remote and alien part of the forest. Suddenly frightened, the tiny Ewok searched the sky desperately for any sign of flying warriors. Then he froze in horror. A hundred yards away, silhouetted against the pale sistermoon, a large mantigrue flew with easy flaps of its big leathery wings, its dangling

forearms and scaly head rising and falling with its wingbeats. How long had it been stalking him? Teebo sadly realized that he had taken no weapon in his excitement to join the hunt. With evil grace, the demon altered its parallel course and closed in on its prey.

Far away, in another part of the forest, the Ewok warriors banked and turned among the trunks of towering trees as the last light of day played on outstretched branches. Below, the Whispering River wound its way through the forest.

"Ready your weapons and be watchful!" shouted Warok. "We approach the Canyons of Mist."

As the rocky walls closed in around them, the warriors rose on gusts of canyon-funneled wind. Soon Warok spotted the gaping mouth of a large cave. Warok, Chief Chirpa, and Pondo landed on a nearby shelf of rock and cautiously approached the cave while the others came to rest on a craggy bluff overhead.

"Malani! Malani, it is I, your father!" called Warok, peering into the hollow blackness, but only his echo answered him.

Chief Chirpa stepped closer and put his sensitive nose in the air. "These caves harbor a too familiar stench," he sniffed. "Duloks have sheltered here."

"And who but a Dulok would devour a lantern bird?" said Warok, pointing to small piles of bones and gray-green feathers.

"Look," said Pondo, indicating loops of stranglevine arranged carelessly on the rock shelf. "Freshly laid snares. A Dulok may yet dwell within."

From the darkness of the cave came a deep growling voice like rolling boulders. "A Dulok? No! Not a Dulok! The king of all the Duloks."

The voice so startled Pondo that he almost stepped backward off the cliff. The Ewoks' eyes searched the dark. A swaying glimmer of three green lights came forward from the gloom.

"Away with you!" growled the voice. "This is no rest perch for fuzzy imps. You trespass on the veranda of King Ulgo the Magnificent. Away! Away!"

The shadowy figure emerged. His light source was a crude wooden cage in which were crowded three beautiful lantern birds, their long tail pods glowing a soft apple-green. In his other hand the wizened, bent old Dulok held a long-handled flint axe.

"Forgive us, your majesty," said Chief Chirpa, "but another Dulok king by the name of Vulgarr cited your cave as being the lair of a fearsome beast."

"Wah, hah!" cried Ulgo, glowering at the three Ewoks. "Vulgarr is a moon-headed fool. I once traded him two scrawny birds for this fine fur vest."

Warok, Chirpa, and Pondo stared wide-eyed with horror. The vest was made of Ewok fur.

"Slay him!" cried Pondo. "He is evil. He turns the skin of our people into a filthy cloak." Pondo stepped forward with lance raised, but Chirpa held him back by his wing brace.

Ulgo hissed and spit. "Back, hairy vermin, before I have you made into a foot wipe."

Warok, his anger rising in him, stepped close to Ulgo. "We go our way to search for my daughter, but first . . .

lantern birds are servants of the Spirit, and sacred. They must always be free." Warok grabbed the cage.

"No!" cried Ulgo. "My breakfast!" The mangy Dulok raised his axe and lunged for Warok, who sidestepped and swung aside, protecting the birds. Warok's main wingspar struck Ulgo's head and sent him stumbling. Over the ledge he went with a frenzied scream and much arm flapping. The Ewoks watched in horror as Ulgo plummeted toward the river far below.

"Ulgo will survive," said Chief Chirpa. "He will hit deep water downstream of that large flat rock."

"Thank the Spirit," uttered Warok.

Just then a mighty wind from out of nowhere raced up the canyon. It howled at the rock walls and raised wavelets on the surface of the river. With tremendous force it blew Ulgo off his plunging course . . .

Whack! Ulgo landed in the center of the flat rock. He lay motionless. The wind subsided and all was silent in the deepening dusk. As was the custom when a forest creature died, Chief Chirpa whispered a secret oath.

"Vulgarr has betrayed us," said Warok, "and I fear the worst for my daughter, Malani, and indeed for all of Happy Grove."

"Yes, we were fools to believe the Duloks," said Chirpa. "We're far from home and night is falling. Flying the forest in darkness is deadly. We must pass the night in Ulgo's cave." Warok opened the cage and the three lantern birds flew skyward. But instead of flying away, the birds began to circle above in the indigo sky, crying a strange warbling call. From the treetops and cliffs and distant hills, other lantern birds joined them. Soon there was a great luminous swarm filling the sky.

"Here is our beacon!" shouted Warok. "Their light will guide us safely home." The Ewoks leaped into the cool evening air and formed their airborne procession. The birds flew close overhead, lighting the way home like a ghostly, glowing cloud.

Over a strange and darkening forest, Teebo rocked in his harness in an attempt to lose altitude. The treetops were yet two hundred feet away. The mantigrue floated above, maneuvering from side to side, awaiting the moment to strike. Looking back, Teebo could see the fierce black eyes watching him as the taloned forehands clenched.

Praying a silent oath to his secret tree-name, Teebo tugged sharply on his left wingwarp. The wingtip dipped and splayed and threw Teebo into a rolling spin. Taken by surprise, the flying demon lurched into a flapping dive, overtook his quarry, and struck. The talons tore through Teebo's wings and closed around his shoulder harness. Shrieking in triumph, the demon began to tow Teebo upward. Teebo writhed and kicked the air and pounded the sinewy forearms with his fists to no avail. Releasing the knotted clasp that held the body straps, Teebo twisted and climbed up and over the leading wingspar. With all his strength, he sank his teeth into the bony wrists. With a screech of shock, the demon kicked free and released the wing, but the talons caught, tearing a gaping hole. The wing fell, tumbling, with Teebo clinging to the struts. Again the demon dove in pursuit, screaming with rage. Teebo saw the black fingers of the treetops reaching up for him. He closed his eyes and braced for the clawing of outstretched branches, but down he fell, past the treetops, down into the utter darkness of the forest at night. With a crash of splintering wings, Teebo landed in a big thicket of wigglewood. He crawled free into a tiny clearing. Above, the demon circled in anger. Teebo wondered at the dense ceiling of foliage. It was almost as if the branches had parted to let him pass, then closed behind him.

Cautiously Teebo surveyed his surroundings. The sistermoon climbed behind racks of gray, scudding clouds. A chill wind stirred the carpet of leaves. Beyond the near circle of trees, the darkness was deep and silent. Teebo could see no farther than a few yards in any direction, and all directions looked the same. He imagined the night crowded with vast shapes that watched him from just beyond the clearing.

Desperately Teebo tried to remember the lessons the elders had taught him. He searched the patterns of stars overhead. Which stars formed the flying snake whose eyes looked north? Teebo stumbled over a bellberry bush. Did the blossoms point east or west at sunset? Or was it sunrise? Which branches did the elders say were best for fire starting? Teebo suddenly felt very small and foolish.

From the depths of the darkness a distant rhythmic rustle, like dozens of feet marching the forest floor, reached Teebo's ears. Pulling a broken strut from the wreckage of his wings, he crouched in a bed of scrubwort. Through the trees he watched three tall black shapes approach on a winding forest path. The sistermoon broke through clouds and shone on waxy red skin and upward-curling fangs. Yuzzums! Teebo sank lower into the shrubbery and lay stone still. The Yuzzums rode spindly spider creatures nine feet tall with luminous yellow clusters of searching eyes.

At the wigglewood bush, the procession stopped. The lead Yuzzum poked the brush with a long forked lance while the spider things slowly looked this way and that. One of the creatures seemed to be staring right at Teebo. It began to sound a low hissing moan. Teebo trembled and tried to sink lower into the scrubwort. A twig snapped under him. Suddenly three clusters of yellow eyes stared at him!

Teebo leaped from his hiding place and ran with all his strength through the darkness. Over logs, through burr brush, between trees, he ran. He looked back and saw three shadowy loping shapes, each with its sulfurous clump of eyes, weaving through the murk.

Teebo burst from the trees into a large meadow. The grass underfoot shone like silver in the wan moonlight. With his breath rasping in his throat, Teebo made desperately for the far bank of the woods. Unhindered by the trees, the spider things gained rapidly. The Yuzzums vented raucous cries and steadied their lances. Teebo could hear the pounding of spider feet almost at his back. "The woods are too far away," he thought, tears streaming from his eyes. A lance whistled past his furry ears and into the grass as he felt the panting spider breath on his neck. With the last of his strength, the tiny Ewok ran for two trees that stood apart from the rest.

All at once, one of the trees seemed to uproot itself and jump right in front of Teebo. He ran headlong into it, but to his surprise found it covered with long thick fur instead

of bark. Dazed, Teebo watched the spiders retreating in three directions, the Yuzzums clinging tightly and howling in terror. Then Teebo saw the source of the Yuzzums' fear. The tree trunks were not tree trunks at all but thick hairy legs. A hand as big as Teebo reached down and grabbed him as he tried to flee. With his head sticking out of the great furry fist, Teebo rode up into the night air. A face loomed overhead. Blinking black eyes, the size of Teebo's head, inspected him. Bucket-sized nostrils flared and sniffed, and a cavernous mouth curled into an enormous grin. The Grudakk!

Teebo was dropped into a pouch of woven vine. He struggled and wrenched but the pouch held firm. The creature turned and made his way into the woods.

Teebo sank to the bottom of his mobile prison in fear and misery. "Now my parents have two children to mourn," he thought, feeling stupid and ashamed. Through the coarse weave of the swinging pouch, Teebo watched tree after tree pass in the moonlight. His captor entered a grove so thick that path and trees merged into shapeless gloom.

The path began a downward slope as the deafening footfalls echoed off surrounding walls. Straining close to the weave, Teebo saw a giant downward-spiraling tunnel ahead, with torches stuck into hollows along the way. By right-angled turns, the tunnel opened onto a spacious lair excavated from dark earth. Roots protruded from the walls and ceiling. Against one wall of the den stood a massive hearth and chimney of stone slabs. A dying fire glowed under a huge cauldron.

The Grudakk set the pouch on the hearth, then blew the

fire to life and stoked the blaze. Monstrous shadows danced up and down the earthen walls.

Teebo tugged and tore at the bindings, knowing that he was about to be another unhappy ingredient in Ewok stew. "Oh, Great Forest Father," he whispered. "This is Teebo of Happy Grove speaking. I promise I'll never run away from home again; I'll listen to the elders and take verygoodcareofmytree . . ."

Teebo was talking very fast now, because he could see the gleam in the Grudakk's eye as he reached down for his pouch.

"I'll never play tricks on my little sister. I'lldoallmychoresI'll—AAAAAAAHHHHHH!" Teebo's prayer was cut short as the Grudakk upended the pouch into his hand. Huge fingers closed around the tiny struggling form. The hand moved toward the cauldron. Teebo would be boiled alive! Tears rolled down the fur of his face. Looking down, Teebo could see the bubbling surface of the stew. He could feel the rising steam. And then the Grudakk's immense face was there, eyes staring, great nostrils sucking tendrils of steam. The creature's other hand held a small branch, carved flat and scooped out at one end. He dipped the branch in the stew and raised it to his mouth. Pursing his lips, he blew carefully, cooling the branchful of stew.

"He's going to taste it," thought Teebo, "to see if it needs another Ewok!" Blinking with tears, he began to wail.

With a smile, the Grudakk popped the homemade spoon into Teebo's mouth. His wailing stopped short and he blinked in total bewilderment. The stew tasted of wild

lichen and mushrooms and sprigmelon, but not at all like stewed Malani.

But then another thought occurred to Teebo. If Malani wasn't in the stew, she'd already been eaten! Teebo thought of his little sister with her straw doll and the red feather in her hood. He began to wail again. The Grudakk was ready with another spoonful. This time Teebo could taste watermoss and bellberries. The stew was really quite delicious.

Between Teebo's wailing and the Grudakk's spooning, the little Ewok consumed a hearty quantity of stew.

Presently the Grudakk tucked his prisoner into a hollowed-out log lined with fur and set the little makeshift bed on the hearth. The glowing embers warmed Teebo's tired feet. With a huge yawn and a pat on the head for Teebo, the Grudakk curled up on a bed of straw. Teebo watched him in the ruby light of the waning fire.

"He's going to keep me for a pet," thought Teebo. "I'll escape as soon as he goes to sleep."

In seconds the Grudakk was snoring deeply. "Maybe I'd best wait until it's light out," Teebo thought, snuggling down deep in the fur blankets. "I'll stay awake all night and escape as soon as I hear the first dawndaddy." Teebo wiggled his toes close to the glowing embers and very soon was sleeping the deep numbing sleep of total exhaustion.

The day dawned gray and dismal over Happy Grove. Logray the medicine man stood somberly at the center of a circle of sullen Ewoks, their heads hung in mournful silence.

Logray raised his eyes to the heavens. In his hand he held the most sacred object of Ewok magic: a branch from the Father Tree. Withered and brittle with age, it had been taken from the primal tree when the moons were young, in a time known only in legend. Logray raised the branch high and began to chant an ancient, desperate oath:

"O Tree, our Father, old as moons,
Listen to our plea.
Lead our spirits when we meet
Our deadly enemy.

Oh, hear your children, Mother Land.
Help make us brave and bold.
The foe who means your children ill
Is strong and hard and cold.

Your family calls, O Brother Sky,
For battle must be done.
Fair winds to be our guiding eye
To keep our family one."

One by one, the Ewoks took up the chant. The warriors raised their weapons to the sky; the mothers held branches from each of their children's trees. Soon the grove was echoing with a hundred Ewok voices. The wind rose and circled around and around the village. Louder and louder the Ewoks chanted and faster raced the wind, until its howling seemed to take up the sacred chant.

All at once a spiraling gust of wind whipped the

branches from the mothers' hands and sent them circling skyward. Boiling clouds parted to admit the little dancing clot of branches, and from the sky above came a light. Not sunlight or morning glow but a light of dazzling brilliance to illuminate the little village and suffuse each Ewok spirit with a strange and wonderful radiance.

All chanting ceased. The Ewoks stood dazed. Only old Logray smiled a small smile of past things remembered. The branch in his hand was supple and green and bursting with new life.

No words were spoken. Each warrior made ready his wings and weapons and filed toward the launchway. The sun peeked over the far hills and began its climb into a cloudless blue sky.

Teebo awoke with a start and looked around. Dusty yellow light was filtering down the tunnel, ashes lay cold and dead on the hearth, and the Grudakk was nowhere to be seen. Teebo threw off his blankets and raced for the earthen stairway. He clawed his way up each Grudakk-sized step. Finally, blue sky and misty shafts of sunlight came into view. Just a few more steps.

Then a massive lurching shape blocked Teebo's view of freedom. Down the steps came the Grudakk. Teebo pressed himself into a corner as the enormous feet passed by. The Grudakk carried a basket of fruit and lichen and his pouch was stuffed with mushrooms.

Teebo scrambled up the last few steps and emerged into the forest. Through the dense and shadowy cluster of trees, into soft morning sunlight, he ran. Pausing to get his bearings, Teebo looked back at the Grudakk's lair. It was in the base of the biggest tree Teebo had ever seen. Its girth was as wide as his village, and its high crown disappeared into the upper haze. Birds of every description flew among branches that were alive with the chirping of young. Teebo thought he heard another sound as well, one that reminded him of the tree songs of his home grove. His heart ached to hear the soft sweet sound from a time that seemed years past.

With a crash of underbrush, the Grudakk emerged from the mouth of his lair, his eyes searching right and left. Teebo turned and ran as fast as his legs would carry him. Over hills he ran, down into a shaded valley, through a bubbling stream and up another hill.

Teebo stopped in a clump of ferns to catch his breath and listened for the thump-thump of an approaching Grudakk. Instead he heard distant voices.

Teebo couldn't hear words, but there seemed to be an argument in progress. He crept cautiously in the direction of the voices and presently came to the edge of a wide meadow. In the center of the meadow were about sixty Duloks breaking camp. Nearby was a ramshackle wagon covered in a patchwork tarp of animal skins. Watching from behind a tree, Teebo recognized the leader, Vulgarr, arguing with another big blue-gray Dulok with a crooked tail.

"As king, I have decreed that we dine here and now!" shouted Vulgarr.

"You've been king too long!" yelled Crooked Tail as he picked up a short stone axe and stepped toward Vulgarr.

One of Vulgarr's henchmen came from behind and crashed a gnarly club down on Crooked Tail's head. The argument settled, Vulgarr rushed to the concealed wagon with a chuckle of glee. He jerked the cover away.

Teebo gasped. There, stuffed in the rickety cage and blinking in the morning light, were all the children of Happy Grove. The youngest ones whimpered as Vulgarr

drooled and wrung his hands. "Behold the picnic of a lifetime," the Dulok king said with an evil laugh. "We'll have them fried and frizzled and braised and sizzled, stewed and simmered and grilled." He jerked open the cage door. "Ah, and here's a choice and tender one," he said, reaching inside. Suddenly he screamed in pain and yanked back his hand; attached to it was little Malani, her teeth firmly clamped onto his thumb. Vulgarr howled and danced in a circle, falling over Duloks and campfires and swinging the tiny Ewok overhead.

Teebo stared in relief and confusion from the edge of the meadow. "The Duloks kidnapped Malani . . . and all the other children!" His brain whirled. He had to save them.

Two of Vulgarr's minions finally pulled Malani loose and held the kicking, scratching furball at arm's length. Vulgarr stepped close, nursing his reddened thumb. In his good hand he held Crooked Tail's axe, and revenge was in his eye.

Teebo stepped into the meadow and hurled a stone with all his might. It struck Vulgarr in the shoulder just as he raised the axe. Vulgarr spun around with a roar of rage, to see Teebo ducking back into the undergrowth.

Before Vulgarr could shout a command, a branch fell out of the clear blue sky and hit him squarely on the head, then another and another. Branches were falling all over the camp. The Duloks stood mystified. When the branches stopped falling, a bone-chilling wind blew out of the forest and raced through the camp, stinging eyes and buffeting ears with icy gusts. As the wind whipped across the meadow it seemed to moan in a deep and ancient voice of woe. The Duloks looked around uneasily.

"We'll move on," said Vulgarr. "This meadow is bewitched." The Duloks hurried around scooping up belongings, glancing fretfully at the sky. "And you, you'll be my midday meal," said Vulgarr to the struggling Malani as he flung her back into the cage.

With a yell, one of the Duloks pointed in the direction of the sudden storm. Riding the wind were thirty Ewok warriors, banking and braking to earth at the far end of the meadow.

The cage of young Ewoks shook with cheers and Teebo's heart leaped for joy. In the front line was his father, Warok. The warriors shed their wings and advanced on foot.

"To the cage!" shouted Vulgarr. "They'll not use arrows with their young so near."

The Duloks took up positions in front of the cage. Dropping their useless bows, the Ewok warriors brought forth spears and short stone swords. At a command from Chief Chirpa, they broke ranks and attacked. Yelping like banshees, they charged toward the Duloks, a few of whom became unnerved and fled.

At once Vulgarr seized a burning branch from one of the campfires and approached the cage.

"Halt, Ewoks, and feast your eyes!" he shouted. Vulgarr thrust the torch through the bars of the cage to elicit screams from within. Horrified, the Ewoks froze in their tracks, still forty yards from the wagon.

"Retreat, warriors!" cried Vulgarr. "Else here and now I roast these bratlings!"

Teebo saw his chance. He broke from his cover and ran like the wind for the battlefield. Dodging a retreating

Dulok, he grabbed a stone axe and reached the rear of the wagon cage. He leaped and clung to the bars, and with as fierce a blow as he could muster, he cracked the hardwood hasp of the cage door.

"Run for the woods!" shouted Teebo.

The heavy door swung down with a flood of escaping woklings, pinning Teebo to the ground. The frantic children disappeared into the surrounding forest.

Again the Ewok warriors charged. Dodging arrows and spears on the run, they gained the campground, where a furious battle began.

"Protect King Vulgarr the all powerful!" shouted Vulgarr as he crawled under the wagon. "Duloks victorious!"

Outnumbered two to one, the Ewoks fought as beings possessed. Most engaged two Duloks, a weapon in each hand. Warok and Chirpa fought back to back, fending off the spears and clubs of five Duloks.

Just as Teebo struggled free of the heavy door, a bony hand grabbed his ankle. Teebo looked down into the wild red eyes of Vulgarr. The evil Dulok gurgled with wicked glee as he pulled the frantic Teebo closer.

The misty air filled with cries of pain and victory, the crash of stone on stone, and the eerie moaning of the wind. Fallen Duloks littered the meadow. As the odds neared one to one, more Duloks dropped their weapons and ran for the woods.

With a viselike grip on the scruff of Teebo's neck, Vulgarr crawled free of the wagon and hoisted him kicking and twisting into the air.

"Behold, Ewoks!" cried Vulgarr as he produced a short

stone knife and held it to Teebo's neck. "Drop your weapons and pull back, or you'll take this one home in two baskets!" He pressed the point of his knife to the furry throat. All fighting stopped as the Ewok warriors looked to Chirpa.

"Set free the little one," said the Ewok chief. "We will go our way. Too much blood has spilled."

"This urchin is our safe passage home," said Vulgarr. "Look for him a day's travel north. Pursue us and he dies."

Leaving their fallen comrades, the surviving Duloks formed a tight group with Vulgarr and his struggling hostage at the center and retreated into the woods.

"Gather the children and tend to the wounded, our enemies as well," said Chirpa to his warriors. "Warok, choose ten who are fleet of wing. With luck and fair winds we—"

Suddenly the forest erupted with screaming Duloks. Gaining the freedom of the meadow, they scattered in all directions, dropping weapons and screeching with terror. Lastly came Vulgarr, his legs a gray-brown blur. His frothing mouth opened and closed but no sound came out. Slipping and stumbling, he zigzagged across the meadow. Then, with a crash of undergrowth and a parting of branches, the Grudakk emerged. In one hand he held Teebo. With the other he stuffed three Duloks into his woven shoulder pouch. Ewok and Dulok alike bolted and ran for cover.

In three gargantuan strides the Grudakk overtook Vulgarr and scooped him up, all the while bellowing in rage.

Warok and Chirpa darted forward in a desperate

attempt to free Teebo. Their spears held rigid, the two Ewoks charged the massive legs of the towering creature.

"Hold!" said a familiar voice. Warok and Chirpa turned and were astonished to see Logray hobbling across the meadow. His wings were nowhere to be seen.

In his hand he held the supple branch of the Father Tree. Reaching the feet of the Grudakk, Logray held the branch high. The Grudakk gently handed Teebo down to Warok, who took the child and held him tight. From the forest burst Malani, who ran and jumped into her father's arms next to Teebo.

The wind died and all was silent in the meadow. From the edge of the forest, Ewok warriors and young peeked out and slowly came forward.

As the Grudakk reached for the branch Logray offered him, it jumped from Logray's grasp and flew quivering to the giant hand. The Grudakk held it close for a moment, then pointed into the distance. All the Ewoks looked. There, over a far line of hills, up out of the mist, towered the largest tree of the forest.

"Ewoks, come forward in peace," called Logray, "and share the secret of the Grudakk. Greet the guardian of the Father Tree."

From all around the ring of trees, cheering Ewoks rushed into the meadow to surround the giant Grudakk. As they approached he set King Vulgarr on the ground. The evil Dulok stood stiff, his mouth frozen in a silent scream, his arms outstretched. The Ewoks stared, bewildered.

"Plant him ankle deep in the soil of this meadow," said Logray. "He needs no tending. He will grow into a twisted

tree as ugly as the evil within him. If a single creature finds refuge in his branches, this miserable demon will finally have served his world."

With flying warriors leading the way overhead, a happy procession of Ewoks bade farewell to the Father Tree and his guardian and set off for home.

At twilight the Ewok village began to echo with song and cheerful voices. Families danced around blazing bonfires and held close their loved ones.

Weakened by the day's labors, Logray slipped away from the celebration. His time was near. Very soon his spirit would fly high to join the flowing rivers of soft color. He climbed slowly onto a high walkway and watched the beckoning sky and listened to the talking of the trees, and there he quietly came upon Teebo in his well-worn perch.

"Are the colors not beautiful?" whispered Logray.

Teebo turned in surprise. "You can see them too?" he asked, his face bright with wonder.

Their eyes met for a long moment, there in the last golden light of day.

"Come with me," said Logray, taking the tiny hand in his own. "There is much to learn."